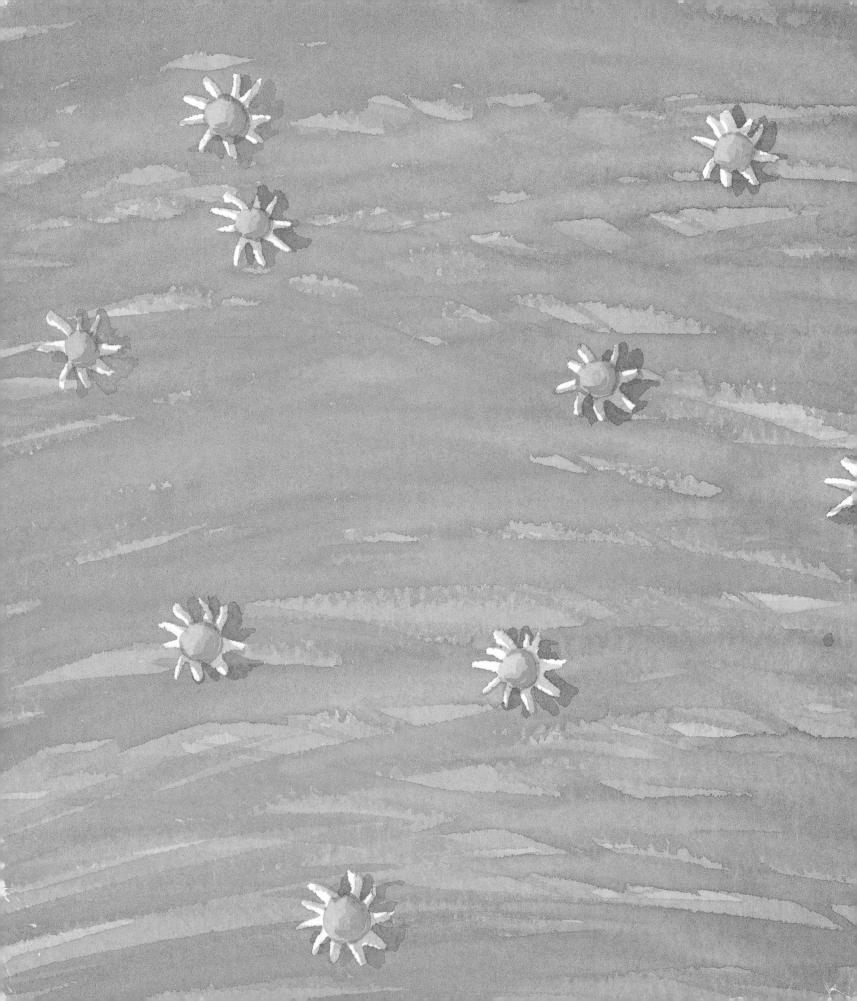

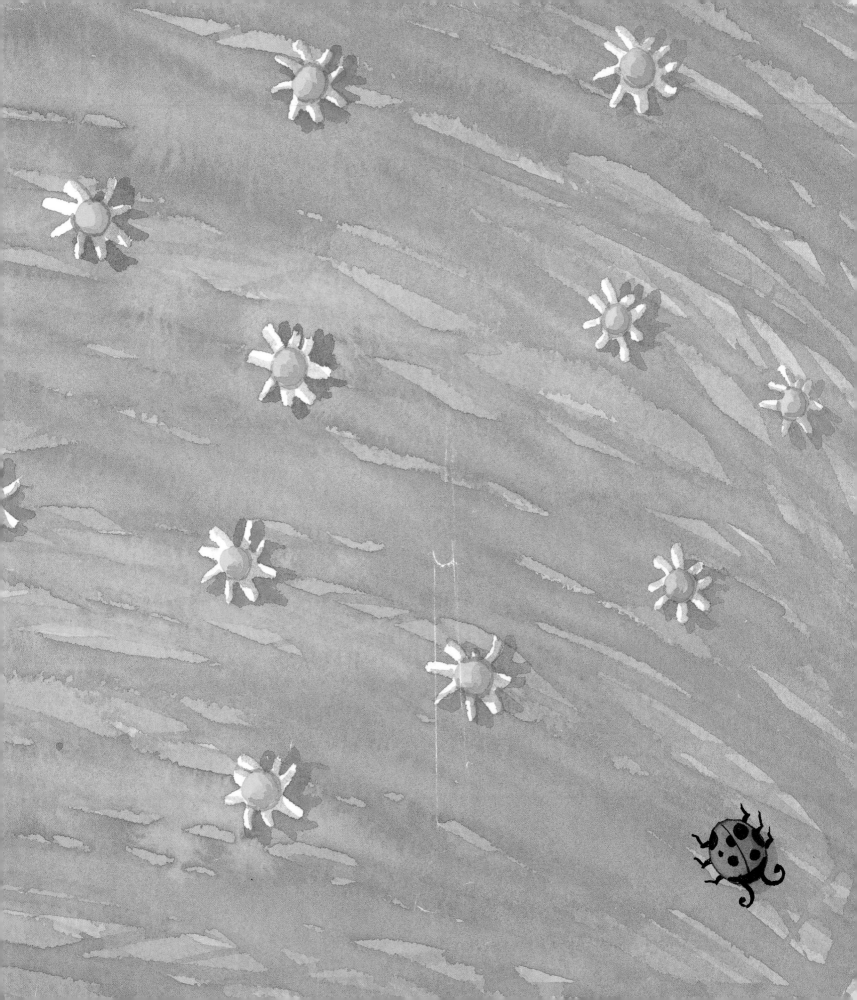

for my daughters —
in amazement and with love

ORCHARD BOOKS
96 Leonard Street, London EC2A 4XD
Orchard Books Australia
32/45-51 Huntley Street, Alexandria, NSW 2015
ISBN 1 84121 038 2 (hardback)
· ISBN 1 84121 270 9 (paperback)
First published in Great Britain in 2002
First paperback publication in 2003
Text and Illustrations © Debi Gliori 2002
(hardback) 10 9 8 7 6 5 4 3 2 1
(paperback) 10 9 8 7 6 5 4 3 2 1
Printed in Dubai

Debi Gliori

Flora's Flowers

ORCHARD BOOKS

Spring is here

and Flora's family are very busy.

Norah planted a huge amaryllis.

Cora planted twenty pink tulips.

"Careful, Flora," said her sisters.

Sam sowed
lettuces,

Tom sowed
sunflowers,

and Max sprinkled cress
on his facecloth.

"Don't touch, Flora,"
said her brothers.

"Why don't you grow something?" said Flora's Dad.

"Some pretty flowers?" said Flora's Mum.

Flora planted a small brick.
"I'm growing a house," said Flora.

"Your brick isn't going to grow as fast as my cress," said Max.

"Or as well as my lettuce," said Sam.

Up sprang Cora's tulips and Norah's amaryllis grew and grew and grew...

"How's your brick, Flora?" said Norah and Cora.

"It's **not** a brick, it's a house," muttered Flora.

Every night for a week, they had Sam's lettuces with a garnish of Max's cress.

"How's your brick, Flora?" said Tom.
"It's **not** a brick, it's a **house**,"
sniffed Flora.

Norah's amaryllis burst open and Cora's tulips were beautiful.

Flora prodded her house hopefully.

Flora put her house outside
beside Tom's spectacular sunflowers,
but still nothing happened.

"I think your brick's dead, Flora," said Sam.

"It's **NOT** a **BRICK!**" wailed Flora. "**IT'S A HOUSE!**"

Winter came, and snow fell.
Nothing grew - inside or out.

Then one day, Spring came back, and Flora's family emerged from their burrow.

"LOOK", yelled Flora.
"MY HOUSE!"

For Flora's brick
had grown...

...into a perfect house.

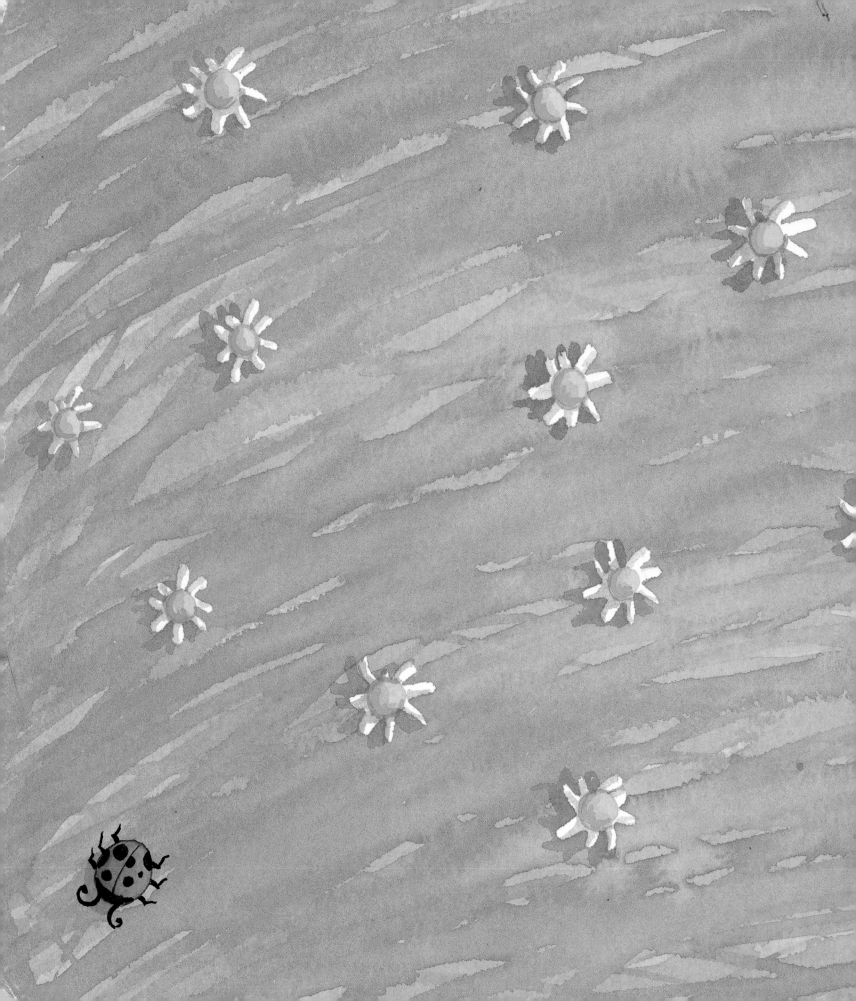